The Littlest Reindeer

Written by
Brandi Dougherty

Illustrated by
Michelle Lisa Todd

Cartwheel Books
An Imprint of Scholastic Inc.

For my editor, Celia. Thanks for loving
these books as much as I do! — B.D.

For my sister, Helen. Now that we've grown up,
I'm quite glad to have you around. — M.L.T.

Scholastic Inc., 557 Broadway, New York, NY 10012
Scholastic UK Ltd., Euston House, 24 Eversholt Street, London NW1 1DB, United Kingdom

ISBN 978-1-338-15738-3

16 15 14 13 12 11   20 21

Printed in the U.S.A.   40
First printing, October 2017

Designed by Jess Tice-Gilbert

Dot was a reindeer.
She lived with her family at the North Pole.
There were many reindeer in Santa's Village,

but Dot was the littlest one.

Dot had a friend named Oliver.
He was the littlest elf in Santa's Village!
Dot and Oliver were Santa's special helpers.
But Dot wanted another job, too.

More than anything, Dot wanted to help fly Santa's sleigh.
Santa would be choosing a new reindeer soon, and Dot was excited.
She just needed a few lessons, and then she would be ready.

Dot's sister, Stina, showed her how to get a running start. Dot's cousins watched, too. "Faster! Faster!" they chanted.

But Dot's short legs just couldn't keep up.
"I bet Carl can help," Stina said comfortingly.

Then Dot's brother, Carl, showed her how to make the first leap into the air.
"It's called the takeoff," he said.
"Okay, now you try," Carl told Dot.

Dot tried with all her might
to jump in the air.
Carl laughed. "Very funny, Dot.
Now really jump this time."

"That was it," Dot whispered.
"Oh …" Carl said. "Well, maybe
Grandpa has some suggestions!"

Dot's grandpa was in the stable. "I need help jumping!" she told him.
"I know exactly what to do!" he said.
Dot's grandpa showed her how to jump from the stable loft and fly.
"Kick, kick, kick!" he shouted.

But when Dot tried to jump off the platform, she sank right into the big hay pile below.

Dot's grandpa pulled her out.
"Why don't you go talk to your mama?"

Dot's mama was at the supply store.
She was picking up a new harness made especially for Dot.

But when Dot tried it on, the harness slipped right off.

"We can fix it!" Dot's mama said.
But Dot shook her head. "I'm too little. I can't run. I can't jump. I can't fly."
Dot's mama nuzzled in close. "But you will soon. There's always next year."

Dot clopped through Santa's Village.
She was sad.
Would she ever be big enough to help fly Santa's sleigh?

Just then, Dot's friend Oliver appeared at her side.
"What's the matter?" Oliver asked.
"I'm too little to fly Santa's sleigh," Dot said.
"But you're not too little to do lots of other things!" Oliver replied. "Come on!"

Dot and Oliver made a snowman.

They played tag with their friend, Charlie.

They made Christmas cards for their families.

And they even helped a baby fox find his mama.

At the end of their busy afternoon, they collapsed in a snowbank to rest.
"See," Oliver said. "Look at all the things we can do!"
Dot smiled. She felt better already.

Before Dot knew it, Christmas Eve had arrived.
The entire North Pole came out to send Santa and the reindeer off
on their important journey. Dot's grandpa gave her a big nuzzle.
"This will be you next year," he said.
Dot nodded.

Everybody cheered and waved as the reindeer got their running start.

But then Dot noticed a tiny present in the snow.
It had fallen out of Santa's bag!

Oliver looked at Dot. "Go, go!" he cried.
Then she picked up the gift and ran as fast as she could.
Just as the reindeer lifted Santa's sleigh into the air, Dot jumped!

It was her highest jump ever as she kicked her legs as hard as she could.
Suddenly, she was flying! She leaped right into the sleigh.
Santa smiled. "Well done, Dot."

When Dot returned to the North Pole early the next morning with Santa and the other reindeer, the whole village was waiting.

Everyone surrounded Dot with hugs and cheers.

"I knew you could do it!" Oliver cried.

Dot finally found a way to help Santa and his sleigh.
Sometimes little is the perfect size after all.
But even better, having a friend by your side
makes anything possible!